The Mess Detectives Case #374: The Big Sleepover

Written by Doug Peterson
Illustrated by Ron Eddy and Robert Vann

BIG IDEA
BOOKS®

Zonderkidz

www.bigidea.com

Zonder**kidz**.

The children's group of Zondervan

www.zonderkidz.com

The Mess Detectives: Case #374 – The Big Sleepover
ISBN: 0-310-70736-6
Copyright © 2004 by Big Idea, Inc.
Illustrations copyright © 2004 by Big Idea, Inc.
Requests for information should be addressed to:
Zonderkidz, Grand Rapids, Michigan 49530

Written by: Doug Peterson
Editor: Cindy Kenney
Illustrations and Design: Big Idea Design
Art Direction: Karen Poth

Printed in China
04 05 06 07/LP/4 3 2 1

ROCKFORD'S FILE

"Anyone who hides his sins doesn't succeed. But anyone who admits his sins and gives them up finds mercy."
Proverbs 28:13 NIrV

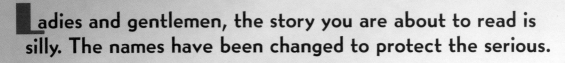

Ladies and gentlemen, the story you are about to read is silly. The names have been changed to protect the serious.

It was a hot Saturday morning in Bumblyburg. Temperatures were already in the low '90s. Even the ice cubes were sweating.

My partner and I were working the Mess Desk. My name is Larry. I'm a detective. I'm also a cucumber. My partner is Bob the Tomato. He carries a badge. I carry a badger.

Don't ask why.

8:33 a.m.

We got an urgent call from Madame Blueberry on the south side of town. She was baby-sitting a group of Veggie friends, who had held a sleepover the night before. They left a major mess. So what else is new?

8:46 a.m.

Bob and I reached Madame Blueberry's
house, which was as hot as an oven. Broken
air conditioner, I guess. Madame Blueberry looked
very upset. She was baking a pie.

"Good morning, ma'am," I said. "My name is Larry the Cucumber,
and this is my partner, Bob the Tomato. He carries a badge. I
carry a badger. Don't ask why."

"Please tell us what happened," said Bob. "Just the facts, ma'am."

Drat. Bob always beats me to that line. "Why do you always get to say, 'Just the facts, ma'am'?"

"I don't always say it," Bob argued.

"Yes you do. I *never* get to say it."

"OK, OK." Bob rolled his eyes. "Go ahead and say it then."

"It's too late," I pouted. "You already said it. You can't say 'Just the facts, ma'am' twice in one adventure. That would be a violation of Section 15, Paragraph 32."

Bob sighed.

"Are you boys done?" asked Madame Blueberry.

"I think so," I said. "So what happened here, ma'am?
Just the—" I stopped myself just in time.

"Percy Pea and some of his friends were having a noisy sleepover upstairs last night," she explained. "They were eating pizza and watching movies."

"Uh-huh," I said. "Go on."

"This morning, when I went upstairs to bring them breakfast, I found the bed was broken. But none of the boys will take responsibility for it. They won't say who bounced on the bed and busted it."

I made a note of that.

9:05 a.m.

We found the four boys in the room upstairs, watching the movie *An American Pea in Paris*. Things were messier than we thought. Dresser drawers were hanging open. Clothes were thrown all over the room.

The bed was badly broken, with one of its legs snapped right off. But three of the boys didn't seem to notice or care. They were eating pancakes on the bed as they rolled off of the tilted mattress. Then they climbed back on. It went on and on. I've seen stranger things, but I can't remember when.

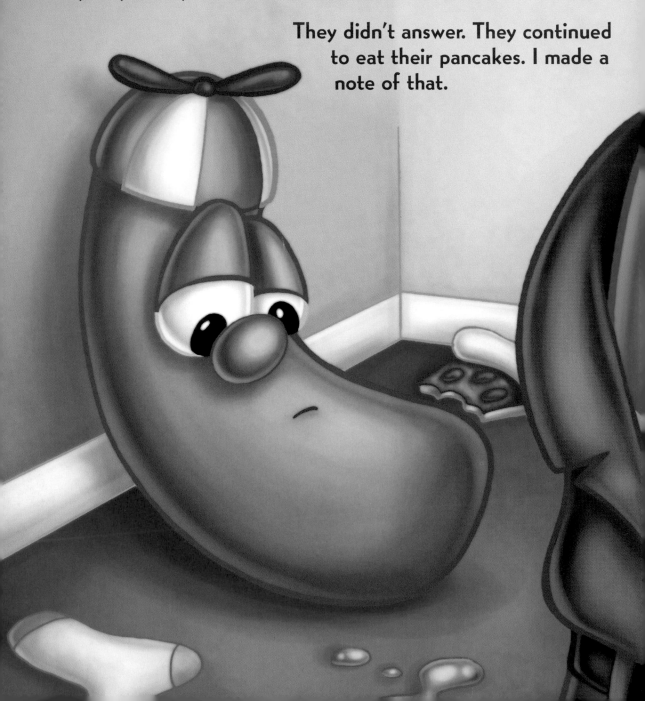

Lenny Carrot was sitting in the corner all alone. He had a strange look in his eyes, but I couldn't put my finger on why. Perhaps it's because I don't have fingers.

"Any of you boys want to tell us who broke the bed?" Bob said.

They didn't answer. They continued to eat their pancakes. I made a note of that.

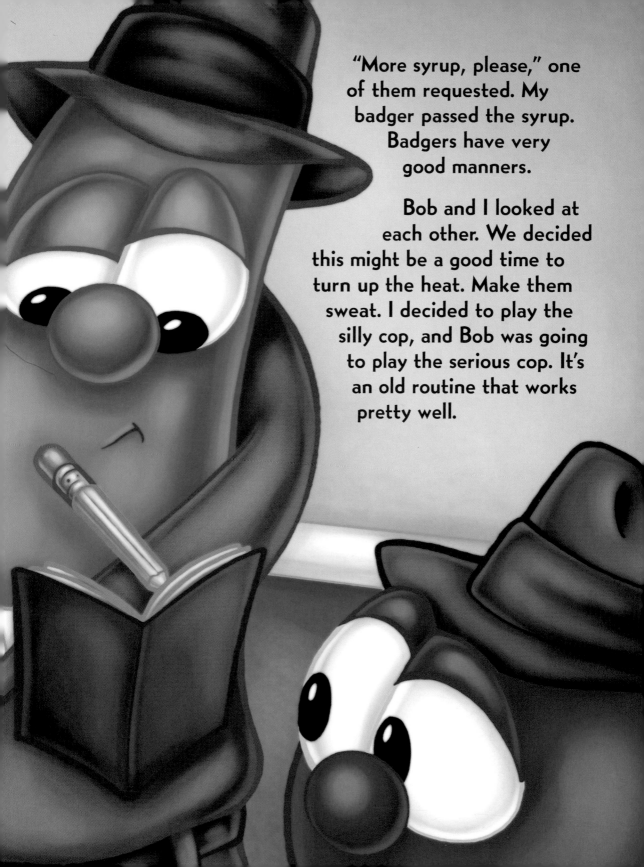

"More syrup, please," one of them requested. My badger passed the syrup. Badgers have very good manners.

Bob and I looked at each other. We decided this might be a good time to turn up the heat. Make them sweat. I decided to play the silly cop, and Bob was going to play the serious cop. It's an old routine that works pretty well.

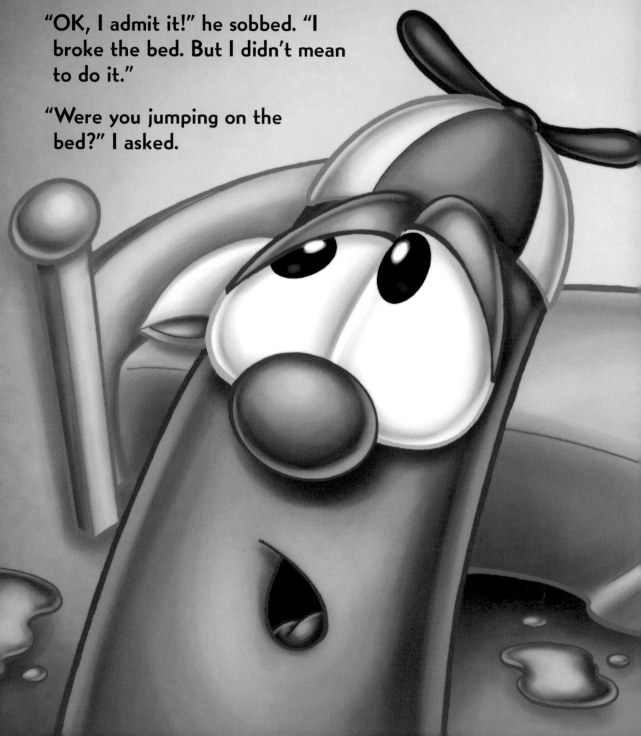

But before we could make a move, Lenny Carrot suddenly broke down.

"OK, I admit it!" he sobbed. "I broke the bed. But I didn't mean to do it."

"Were you jumping on the bed?" I asked.

"NO!" Lenny shouted. "I just sat on the bed, and the leg broke."

"You did the right thing by coming clean about this, Lenny," said Bob. "That's called 'taking responsibility.' Doesn't it feel good to admit it when you mess up?"

Lenny nodded. "I felt terrible hiding that secret."

9:15 a.m.

It looked like this was going to be an open-and-shut case. Bob and I were getting ready to take Lenny downstairs to apologize to Madame Blueberry. But that's when things took a surprising twist.

"I can't stand here and watch Lenny take the heat. He shouldn't take the blame," Percy Pea suddenly blurted out. "Lenny didn't do it."

The other boys gasped. Pieces of pancake flew out of their mouths and onto the floor. (Never gasp with your mouth full.)

"OK, suppose you tell us what happened. Start from the very beginning," I said. "And give it to me straight, man." (I've always wanted to say that.)

"Last night, Lenny went downstairs to help Madame Blueberry get the pizza ready," Percy explained. "While he was gone, the rest of us started jumping on the bed."

"Uh-huh." I made a note of that.

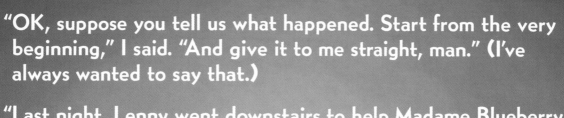

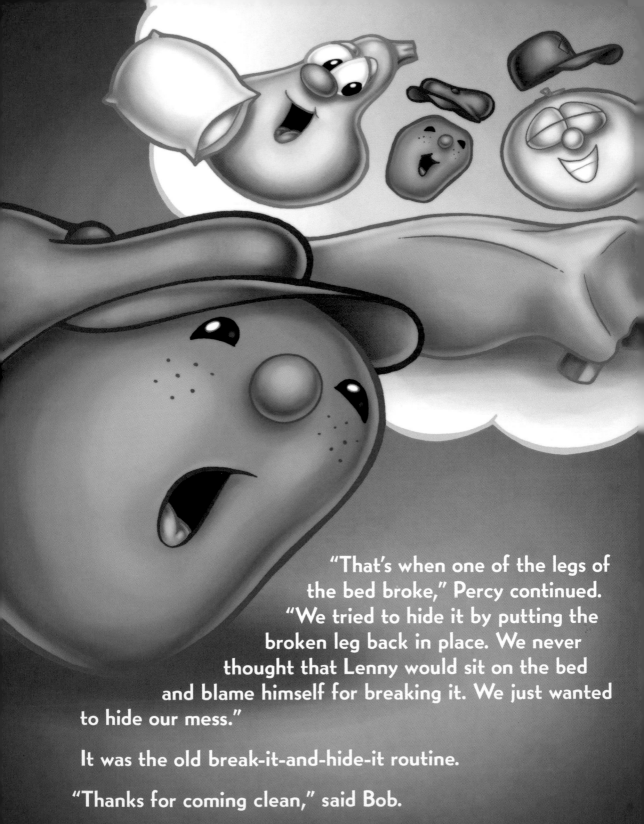

"That's when one of the legs of the bed broke," Percy continued. "We tried to hide it by putting the broken leg back in place. We never thought that Lenny would sit on the bed and blame himself for breaking it. We just wanted to hide our mess."

It was the old break-it-and-hide-it routine.

"Thanks for coming clean," said Bob.

Because of Percy's honesty, the guilty Veggies would probably get an easy punishment—a weekend of being grounded with the hope of parole. It was a typical pea bargain. Once again, it looked like the case was closed.

But things were far from over.

The other boys were burning mad that Percy had spilled the beans. They tried to pin the blame on one another.

"It wasn't my fault!" shouted Harold, looking at Joe. "It was *his* idea to jump up and down on the bed!"

"No! *He* started it!" Joe yelled, glaring at Harold.

"No! *He* started it!" Harold shouted, staring at Joe. "It's not my fault! *He* told me to do it!"

9:36 a.m.

Things were spinning out of control. The boys wouldn't stop shouting. Blame was being thrown around like a hot potato.

That's when it happened. Harold aimed a bottle of syrup at Joe. "This syrup is loaded, and I'm not afraid to use it," he snarled. "Now admit it, Joe. Tell them it was your idea to jump on the bed."

"Cool it, baby!" I shouted. (I've always wanted to say that.) "Don't do anything you'll regret later."

All the other boys picked up pillows.
Then Percy snatched up a second bottle
of syrup. This had the makings of a sticky
situation. My badger crawled under my trench
coat to hide.

"It doesn't matter who started bouncing up and down on the
bed first," Bob said. "You're *all* responsible for what happened.
You *all* need to share the blame. Each one of you boys should
come clean and admit you messed up. You'll feel much better
if you do."

The boys glanced at each other with shifty eyes. Things had never been so tense. My badger's claws dug into my back. I made a note to have them trimmed.

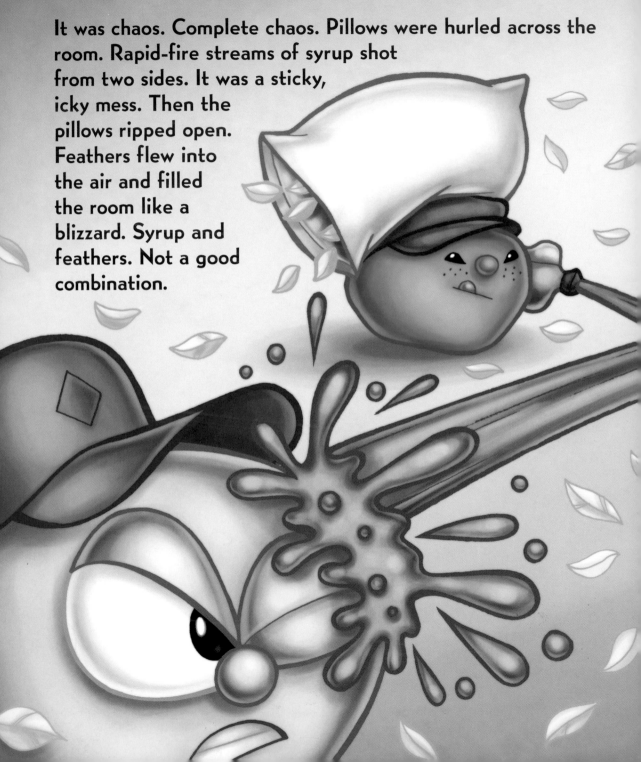

Suddenly, Harold fired a stream of syrup and hit Joe. Joe swung back with his pillow.

It was chaos. Complete chaos. Pillows were hurled across the room. Rapid-fire streams of syrup shot from two sides. It was a sticky, icky mess. Then the pillows ripped open. Feathers flew into the air and filled the room like a blizzard. Syrup and feathers. Not a good combination.

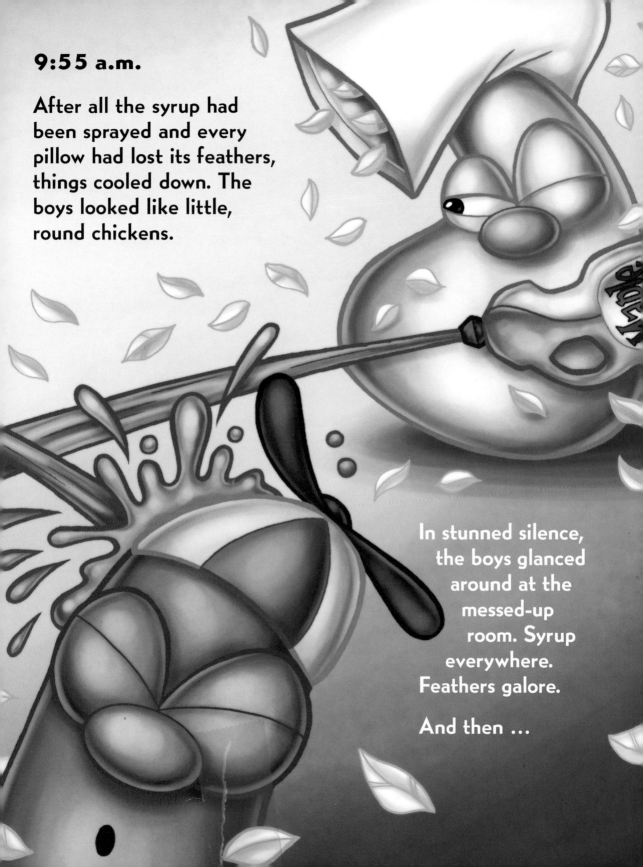

9:55 a.m.

After all the syrup had been sprayed and every pillow had lost its feathers, things cooled down. The boys looked like little, round chickens.

In stunned silence, the boys glanced around at the messed-up room. Syrup everywhere. Feathers galore.

And then ...

"I'm sorry," Harold said, right out of the blue.

Two little words. But they did big things.

"I feel awful," Percy admitted. "This is all my fault."

"No, I was the one who messed up," said Joe. "If I hadn't sprayed the syrup, none of this would have happened."

"No, it's *my* fault," insisted Lenny. "*I* was the one who suggested that we jump on the bed last night. *I* started this mess."

Bob and I couldn't believe our ears. *Everyone* was taking responsibility. For a moment, I thought the boys were going to start fighting over who was more to blame. That's when they all decided to clean up the room. It was another way that they could take responsibility. They wanted to make things right for Madame Blueberry.

"We owe her a big apology," said Percy.

"I appreciate that," said a voice from behind us. We all whirled around to see Madame Blueberry standing in the doorway staring at the mess. She had overheard everything. But did she explode in anger? Did she lose her cool?

No way, José. (I've always wanted to say that.)

Instead, Madame Blueberry took the boys into the backyard and set up the lawn sprinkler. Then, one by one, the boys and my badger ran through the cool, refreshing water. The syrup and feathers washed away in the spray.

The boys felt clean and refreshed, inside and out.

Bob and I watched as the boys played a game of tag in the water. We were happy about everything they had learned today. They learned to take responsibility. They learned to admit when they messed up. And they learned to never play tag with a badger that needs his claws trimmed.

"That sprinkler sure looks good," Bob said.

"Yeah. Trench coats feel awfully hot on a day like this," I agreed.

Bob and I looked at each other.

"You thinking what I'm thinking?" Bob asked.

"Uh-huh."

Bob and I turned and ran through the sparkling water, getting drenched to the core. As we did, Harold accidentally ran into me, knocking me over.

"I'm sorry," said Harold. "My fault entirely. I admit it."

"Don't sweat it, Daddy-O."

I've always wanted to say that.